Humphrey's FIRST CHRISTMAS

Written and Illustrated by Carol Heyer

ideals children's books.
Nashville, Tennessee

ISBN-13: 978-0-8249-5559-5

Published by Ideals Children's Book
An imprint of Ideals Publications
A Guideposts Company
535 Metroplex Drive, Suite 250
Nashville, Tennessee 37211
www.idealsbooks.com

Color separations by Precision Color Graphics, Franklin, Wisconsin
Printed and bound in Italy by LEGO

Library of Congress Cataloging-in-Publication Data

Heyer, Carol, 1950-
Humphrey's first Christmas / Carol Heyer.
p. cm.
Summary: A camel, grumbling about losing his favorite blanket then having to carry a heavy load, meets a special newborn baby who fills him with love, joy, and generosity.
ISBN 978-0-8249-5559-5 (alk. paper)
[1. Camels--Fiction. 2. Jesus Christ--Nativity--Fiction. 3. Christmas--Fiction.] I. Title.
PZ7.H44977Hum 2007
[E]--dc22

2007005824

10 9 8 7 6 5 4 3 2 1

Thanks to Suzan Davis Atkinson and Siri Weber Feeney for their help and support.

To Pat Pingry—my editor, my publisher, and my friend

For my parents, Merlyn M. and
William J. Heyer, now and always

Beloved

Most Beauteous

and Exalted King of All

should be my name.

Instead, they call me . . .

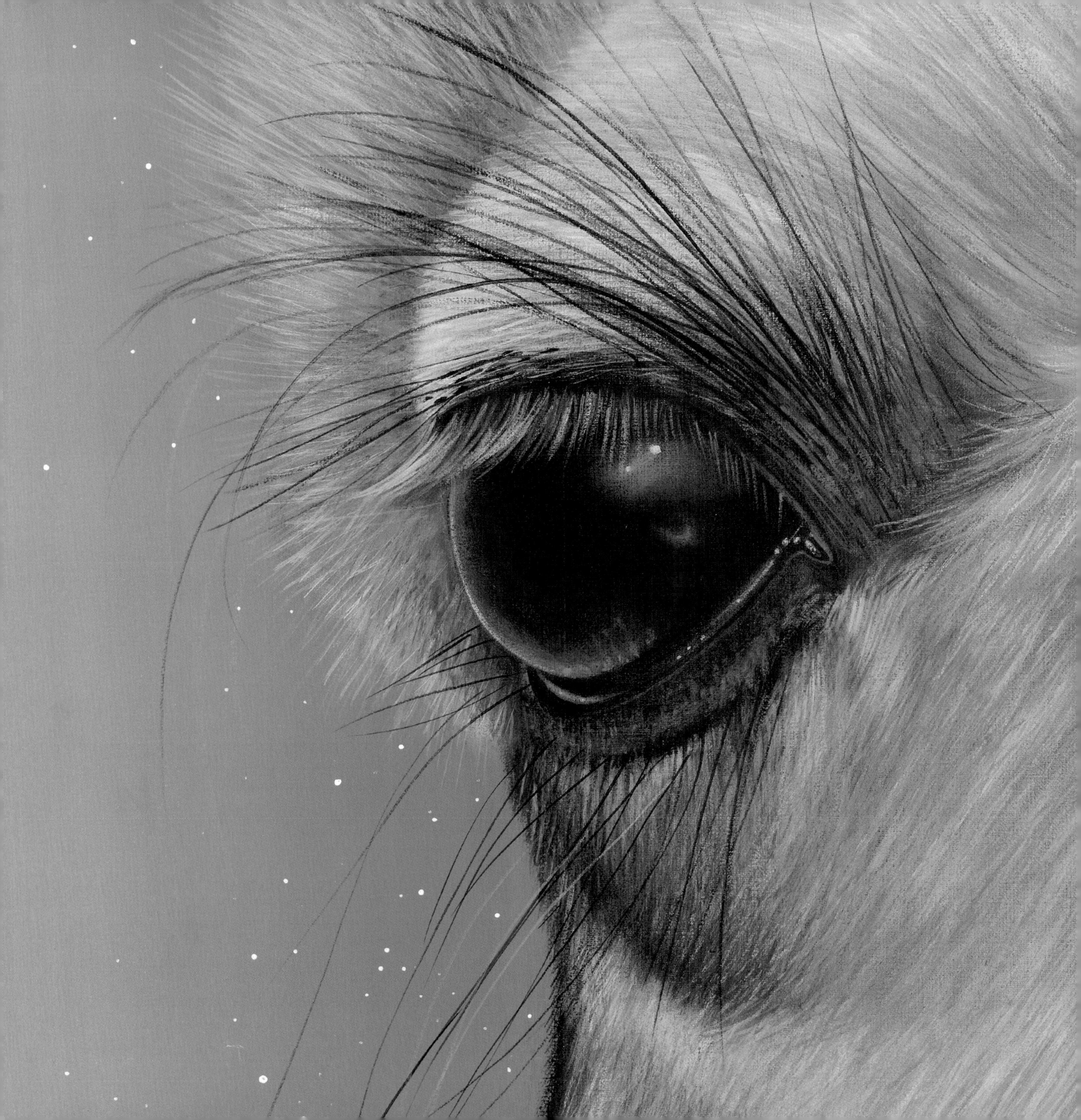

Humphrey!

This I could bear, if the worst thing of all had not happened. My dearest possession, my glorious carpet blanket, has been lost along the trail. Now, I am never warm and I suffer terribly.

That is why I have set into motion a plan to replace my greatest of all treasures.

I carefully nudge my nose inside the caravan master's tent. This is followed closely by the chattering of my teeth, thereby letting the master know that I am most enormously cold.

Success! He has not pushed me out, and I remain hopeful that a new blanket will soon be mine.

Three rich caravans have joined us, and there has been talk of kings. Yet these kings bring me no joy, for they have tied three huge chests to my bare back. They are so heavy, I am sure each must be filled with rocks.

The other camels are wearing the finest of blankets. They are all comfortable and warm. Not one of them thinks about me, their cousin, in pain and misery because of the loss of my most precious carpet blanket.

I cry out in sorrow. I weep.

Today I continue my plan to regain my treasured blanket. I add loud sniffling to the chattering of teeth and squeeze my entire body inside my master's tent.

As I do so, out rolls my master, for the tent is exactly camel-sized.

It is as I planned! As the master chases me away, he tosses me a new blanket. I have success!

Once more I am covered with splendor and comfort. I am filled with delight. If it were not for the heavy chests I am forced to carry, I would be almost happy.

We have followed one star for many long nights. Now our caravan enters the town of Bethlehem. Its streets and inns are crowded with travelers. My master gives no thought to my tired feet and rumbling belly. I am forced to move on.

At last we reach the end of our journey, but I am confused. There is no great palace, no rich oasis, no palms heavy with fruit. I see only a lowly stable with a family inside.

The three kings rejoice and rush forward to bow before the young woman who cradles a baby.

Finally! The chests are taken from my back and placed before this tiny child.

As each box is opened, I see no stones, only gold, frankincense, and myrrh!

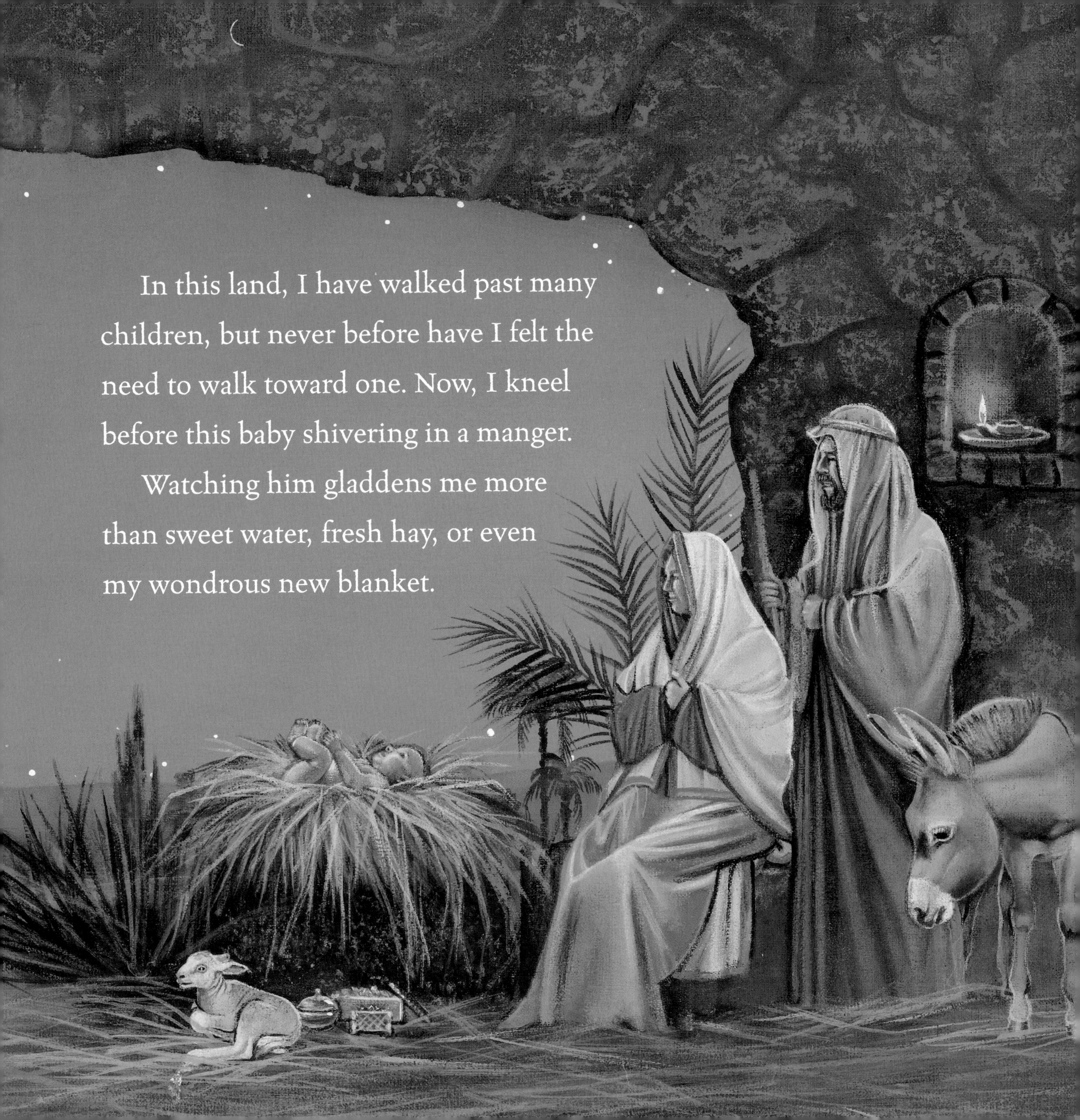

In this land, I have walked past many children, but never before have I felt the need to walk toward one. Now, I kneel before this baby shivering in a manger.

Watching him gladdens me more than sweet water, fresh hay, or even my wondrous new blanket.

I look into the baby's eyes, and I am overwhelmed by love. I pull the treasure from my back and lay my gift carefully upon this child.

He smiles, and my nose and whiskers tingle with joy. I am happy to my toes, and even without my blanket, I feel warm.

Most Beauteous

and Exalted King of All

should be his name.

Instead, they call him . . .

Jesus.